RED NEW DAY & OTHER MICROFICTIONS

Also By Angela Slatter

Collections

The Girl With No Hands and Other Tales

Midnight & Moonshine (with Lisa L. Hannett)

Black Winged Angels

The Female Factory (with Lisa L. Hannett)

A Feast of Sorrows: Stories

Winter Children & Other Chilling Tales

The Heart Is a Mirror for Sinners & Other Stories

Sourdough Stories

Sourdough & Other Stories

The Bitterwood Bible & Other Recountings

Of Sorrow & Such

The Tallow Wife & Other Stories

All the Murmuring Bones (Forthcoming 2021)

Morwood (Forthcoming 2022)

Verity Fassbinder

Vigil

Corpselight

Restoration

RED NEW DAY & OTHER MICROFICTIONS

ANGELA SLATTER

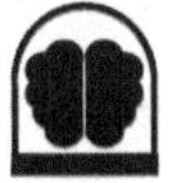

A Brain Jar Press Chapbook
www.brainjarpress.com

Contents

Dedicated to my mother, Betty Slatter, whose voice it was that led me to love stories.

These stories were all written as part of the Daily Cabal web
project some years ago. They appear collected here for the
first time.

A Monkey in the Hand

In retrospect, dear reader, it was a mistake.

I should have known. Mere days after I finished the mech-monkey, I found it dissecting its real-life counterpart. Pinned it to the table with my set of German-engineered scalpels, and taken it apart. The dirigible from Stepney Marsh was running late, so when I arrived home with a sack of new books, the deed was almost done. I should have disassembled it then, but I thought I saw something in its eyes, something *human*. A desire to *know*, to *learn*, to *understand* why it was different to the soft, furry mirror that wailed and squealed and gave up life so quickly.

All I could hear was my father's voice, heavy with disappointment but no real surprise: *Oh, Phineas. You're so careless. Look at the mess you've made.*

So I tidied up the sticky, stinking corpse and threw it down the chute. I listened as it clanged along the shaft, whirled around the spiral bits, thudded into the sharp bends, then came the faint *whomp* as the flames gobbled it up.

I was careful to clean all the bevelled and engraved edges of the mech-monkey, and under his glass nail (which I realised were too sharp by half). I checked his insides to make sure the clockwork mechanisms were all working, not misfiring in a way that might cause a psychotic episode. Turning him around, I opened the little hatch in his lower back where, each morning, I scooped three small loads of coal to feed his tiny internal furnace. The emissions came out as small, popping farts and, if I forgot to open a window, my workshop filled up very quickly with a nasty charcoal smoke.

I kept it—it was useful for fetching and carrying, and it opened cans terribly well. Then one Tuesday I found it reading; it saw me and threw the book away, but it was too late by then. I *knew*.

It probably would have been okay if I hadn't got the next idea. I had been thinking about making a Galatea, but then I read about some sailors who'd caught themselves a mermaid and tried to bring her back to Portsmouth. They kept her in a barrel of seawater on the deck, but it seems she jumped ship just out of harbour, waved goodbye and ducked under the dark, cold sea.

And I thought 'What if?'

Bad Hair Day

"Shoulda worn a better hat," says my sister.

"Yes, thank you," I reply, a little testily. "Hindsight is twenty-twenty."

"Hey, don't get cranky with me. *I* did not do this." She makes a sweeping gesture with her hand.

Stones as far as the eye can see, big and small. Stone *statues*, that is.

"It could have been worse," I venture.

"How precisely?"

I think about it. "I'm not entirely sure, but most things can be worse."

She surveys the damage and sighs. "I guess it could have been a parade or something. Something televised – now *that* would have made this worse."

I'm kinda touched that she's being a bit more supportive than usual. The sisterly solidarity doesn't last though, and she blurts, "But honestly, how did this happen?"

"You said it yourself—hat failure. I wanted a walk in the park," I say. "It was a beautiful day—how often do I get to Central Park? How often do I get anywhere? Getting hunted by heroes puts a bit of a blip in a social life. Anyway, I didn't realise how windy it was."

"You know, every time you want a social life, we have to change address—and it's not just cities, is it? It's countries and continents. And what is it with you and parks, anyway? Can't you be like a normal monster? You know, skulking in caves? The whole hiding thing a bit too hard for you?"

"Easy for you, Stheno, you weren't ever human. You don't know what it was like. You don't know what I lost." I go to kick at a rock at my feet, realise it used to be a Chihuahua and stop.

"And *why* can't you go out at night?"

"A park's not the same a night. Honestly, what have you got for brains?"

We look at the people I turned to stone. "Well, we all have to shift again—Euryale isn't going to be happy. She's still pissed about Stockholm."

"Hey, Stockholm, we got away with—the Millesgården looks amazing."

"You're paying for the move this time. We'd better go via a bookstore and pick up a new atlas, maybe some Lonely Planet guides. Try and find a new city."

"Oh, somewhere with a nice park—"

"Medusa!"

"Okay! Okay!"

Beggar-maid

In this kingdom, even beggars can become something better.

It is a promise that has led us all to this long line of supplicants, waiting for a hot meal and the opportunity to be *chosen*. I stand among the stinking hordes, darkly-hooded, hunched, ignored.

A small man walks the line, making a selection. He reaches me; I straighten, pull the hood back a little; my eyes remain shadowed. He picks up the glimmer of skin, full lips, a finely-boned face.

"You. Follow."

And I do, passing those envious unchosen, through bronze doors, into the great hall, empty as a skeleton's ribcage but for the triple throne. The little man leads me to a small dark door. He ushers me through, does not follow. The door closes with the scratching of a key in the lock, and I am alone in a dimly lit room; alone with the Three.

"Beggar-maid. Now is your chance to become part of *us*, something new," whispers the male. He is well-made, but his skin is puffy. The women are pale, frayed. Obeying the lore, they have not ventured into the sun for a long time. This is no harem; they control him, this whole *spectacle* was their idea.

Trying to infect themselves with gluttonous feasting on cattle-blooded peasants; committing pointless murders when the only thing that will make them like *me* is a bloodline, is *evolution*. It was false piety, foolish games—they didn't think the Blood Mother would rise. But their prayers woke me and rise I did, painfully, unwillingly. I came.

"No," I say. "But it's *your* chance to become something *other*."

My cloak falls back and my wings shake loose. The Three see the full glory of my face, luminous as the moon and framed by black hair, with white-as-snow fangs, red-as-blood lips. The face painted on temple walls; they've seen it so often they've forgotten to fear.

"Stolen blood will not lengthen your lives." My shadow grows, engulfs them.

Their blood is flat, diluted. But it is enough after my centuries of sleep.

The little man enters, later; he heard too many screams. He eyes the finely-dressed husks. He is pragmatic, clever, sees an advantage for himself.

"There will be but one ruler here," I tell him.

He nods. "Yes, my Queen."

"Then bring them to me and choose carefully."

Binoorie

The minstrel made a harp of my sister's bones, polished and shaped them as he needed. He used the silken threads of her hair for strings; plangent, guilt-inducing.

It had seemed such a simple thing to push her over the seawall, to watch her founder and splash and drown. To think that was the end of it all. The wedding day came and I could not feel joy. I took no pleasure in my husband's face, nor in the thought of our life together, of what lay ahead. Each time I looked at him and tried to smile, all I could see was him aging before my eyes, faster and faster, becoming death.

When the minstrel arrived, his strange instrument on his back, I was grateful for the distraction. He plucked at the strings and it seemed they had anchors in my stomach for the noise wrenched at me. He played my shame, for all to witness; my sister's bones singing our story for wedding feast guests to hear.

It was simple enough to take the harp from the minstrel's hands—he gave it up easily, as if he knew it was his only to borrow—and I walked from the hall. I took to the roads, earning my keep with the bones of my sister, singing over and over. I wear my guilt like a cloak, begging forgiveness as a beggar does alms.

My days are cold and lonely, cut adrift from all things that might once have afforded me comfort. Worse still are the nights when she sings me to troubled sleep, her strings moving of their own volition, her voice something that drops through the air like bitter rain. And the sound of the sea, the crash and swell of it just as it was the day I threw her in comes back to haunt me like a refrain.

It would be easy, I suppose, to throw her in once again, to tie something heavy to these polished bones and let her sink into the green darkness; to drown her a second time. But I cannot let her go. I did so once and it was, I now know, my greatest loss. So I keep my penance close, to pierce me like a bone through the heart.

Bone and Breath

They lured me here with promises of marriage. The best of men, the greatest of warriors was to be my husband.

We left my brother and sisters behind, taking the lightest chariot, the fastest horses, my mother and I. Chrysothemis and Elektra wept, covering their faces with grief at our parting, but I saw their eyes, rich and dark with envy. My sisters swallowed down the bitter aloes of my marriage to Achilles, of my being chosen for such an *honour*.

How could we have known? Any of us, stupid girls. Stupid children. Even our mother was deceived.

We came to Aulis where Artemis had stilled the ships, all because my father had hunted sacred deer in the grove. Achilles waited, ardent, he himself taken in by my father's promises.

Agamemnon sold me not for a bride-price but for a breath of wind.

I stepped from the chariot, all white and gold, the loveliest bride a man could hope for (if he could not have bright Helen to wife). My skin was pale, hair shining ringlets, eyes blue as the Aegean, my body ready for my bridegroom's bond.

Father led me past Achilles, spoke to me quietly, told me
it was my *duty*. He led me to the altar where Calchas stood,
dagger in hand; where kindling had been laid in wait to carry
the sacrifice upwards. Achilles wailed, a child deprived of his
new toy, but he conceded soon enough to promises of greater
treasure. Of his pick of the Trojan women.

My mother howled and I wondered for a moment if
perhaps Hera might come to her aid. Might smite them
down, all these men who thought it fair and just to cut short
my life. Clytemnestra would not forgive and her vengeance
would be terrible, but no more than my father deserved.

They speak of me as immortal. They say the goddess took
pity on me and flew me away to Tauris, leaving a white hind
in my place. They say a man there loved me, gave me
children. That I had a long life far from here.

They lie. No god-blood in my veins. I was but flesh and
blood, bone and breath and the blade was cold against my
throat. I am another unhappy shade left to walk the dust of
this earth.

Foresight

I don't want to go in.

He's there now, didn't hesitate. It's his home though he's been away for long years. I warned him, or tried to but who listens to me?

I saw his wife in the shadows just before she stepped through the door, and in that moment she seemed huge, swarming. Then she moved forward, into sunlight and she shone.

Not as beautiful as her sister, but no one is. Tall, broad-shouldered, jaw strong, forehead wide, cheekbones high. Clytemnestra is handsome rather than lovely. She moves with deceptive slowness, but there are muscles evident beneath her rich robes. She's a warrior queen and has not let herself run to fat. Her hair, red-gold in the sun burns like liquid copper.

The smile she gives Agamemnon is frozen; she speaks soft words of welcome and he is deceived. When she looks at me she sees no Trojan princess, merely a slave, hair lank and oily, back and shoulders hunched as if deprived of wings and ashamed of their nakedness.

"Don't go inside," I whispered to my master, my owner,

my thief. In spite of it all, I did not want him to walk all unawares into his fate, for his end means mine. But he gave me an annoyed glare, sick unto death of my constant warnings and plaints, of the sharp dreams that have broken my sleep (and thus his) these past months as we travelled to Argos. He has no patience. He is tired unto death of my madness.

He took his wife's welcome as his due and went in to the bath she had prepared for him. Clytemnestra watched me and nodded slowly before she turned and followed him. I waited, held my breath, counted the beats until I heard him scream, heard the wet sound of a great axe burying itself in muscle and flesh, releasing blood into the air. She waits inside now; another man by her side.

I have seen this for so many days. Fate cannot be avoided. I *am* a Trojan princess. I step down from the chariot, swallowing hard. I put my foot on the first step and mount the portico. My end lies here.

Circe

They ran on all fours, pausing only to sniff the air and howl.

Sometimes they were men, sometimes wolves, always grey though, always hungry. The moon lit their way as they slipped like shadows along the streets. Sometimes they got distracted by trash cans ripe with enticingly decayed odours, but the *other* pulled them on, so they didn't stop for long. Nipper, Gnasher, Fang and Bob.

They had her scent, warm in the cool night air.

Some way after 5th Avenue they caught the sound of footsteps, the click of her heels on the pavement. Familiar and strange, enticing. They followed, kept her in sight, but hung back and stayed in the deep shadows the tall buildings dropped in their wake. She moved from the expensive cantons of the city to the less well-kept, and finally crossed that invisible barrier into the place where slumlords held sway.

Whenever she passed beneath a streetlamp, they could see the red hair and pale skin she flaunted. Long-legged and slim, she was graceful and unaware. The building she approached was dilapidated, seeming to decay before the eye.

A man sat on the stoop, huddled, wrapped in stinking

garments as if the stench might keep the cold away. She smiled and he looked at her, surprised. The woman did not belong.

"Soup," she said, handing him a flask she'd fished out of her coat pocket. "That will warm the back of your soul."

He sniffed at the open mouth of the flask suspiciously. Rich, meaty odours wafted up and made him salivate. He'd have preferred booze, but figured he'd take whatever he could. Lifting the flask in toast to her, he took a mouthful. It was delicious and he made short work of the contents.

The pack had crept close. Surely she could hear rush of their breathing, but she gave no sign. Gnasher gathered his strength and sprang.

She ducked and the wolf sailed over her head.

"Gnasher!" Her voice was stern. "All of you. Sit!"

All four of them, sat, shamefaced at her feet and whimpered. Each one gave a contented sigh when she scratched behind their ears.

"That's better." They pressed themselves against her legs, vying for attention. "Now, say hello to your brother."

On the stoop, a sleek wolf sprawled, looking rather bewildered. He gave a burp and a rich meaty scent wafted out.

"Come, Ulysses. Time for home."

A Complex Elektra

When my sister did not return, I secretly rejoiced.

Clytemnestra came back from Aulis hollow-eyed and silent. She did not speak for many days—her charioteer told my remaining siblings and I what had happened. How our father had sacrificed Iphigenia to buy the wind to give his ships sail. There had been no wedding, no Achilles to husband, no bright future for my oldest sister.

Mother retreated inside herself, refused to eat. For a while I thought she might die, but it showed yet again that I neither knew nor understood she who'd bred me. She fed her anger and grief, and plotted. She practised with the great axe that had been a wedding gift from her own father. In my father's stead she ruled Mycenae and took her husband's cousin to her bed.

Upon his return, Agamemnon breathed the air of his own home for the briefest of times before being slaughtered as he lay in a bath. No matter what the gossip says, it was *she* who wielded the axe, not her lover.

My brother, Orestes, fled; my sister, Chrysothemis, happily remained. I stayed, too, silently disapproving, haunted by dreams and visitations. I knew Agamemnon had not loved me, but I thought if I honoured him in death, his shade might see and bear witness to my devotion.

I helped Orestes hide, wavering fool. When I took food and clean clothes, I spoke of how our mother had offended the very gods. I wore him down, I think, as he grew weary of the isolation, of living in fear, of being deprived of his inheritance. He finally agreed and everything I had planned and set in place was ready. I smuggled him into the palace dressed as a beggar and hid him in my room until day turned into the bruised plum of evening. At last, I handed him the axe our mother had used. Even though she'd cleaned it of our father's blood, still I could see the haze of red on the bright blade.

And I watched my brother walk from the room, waited for the scream. When those came, I nodded to the creatures no one else had seen, waiting on the windowsill. The Furies, silhouetted against the horizon and the wine-dark sea, defiled the skyline. They crowed happily to have their meat.

Foundation

They buried me beneath the foundation, watered the earth with my blood and all my decaying fluids.

They built a hill-fort over me. I held it firm for many years, kept its walls strong against all enemies, protected all those who bore my blood. Listened to them lead lives denied to me. Their time ran out eventually and it didn't matter how bravely I held the walls. The elements took their toll; roofs fell in, walls tilted out of true, stones tumbled.

The earth shifted as the years rolled by. The hill flattened, levelled out, my bones moved with it, my bones and the fine dust particles that had been my clothing and my skin. I let the walls crumble, let the hill sink down; sank down with it myself. There was nothing, no one to care about; no one to protect, no blood calling to mine, no family.

Tired, so tired.

The land lay fallow for a long time, cattle grazed above me, foxes barked, badgers dug, grass grew, died, grew again. A farmhouse was built. The sounds of children startled me out of sleep, making my bones dance with forgotten joy. I loved the foundation once more, reached upward, threaded myself through the floors, walls, stretched my soul across the ceiling, wrapped the home.

Three hundred years passed, six families sheltered inside, each personalising, making it *home*. After the last left (the children grew and flew, the parents stayed until they could no longer negotiate the crooked stairs), the farmhouse lay empty until a new family came: a father, two sad children and a new wife, a not-quite-mother.

I heard the noises of a family uncomfortable with each, trying, learning, failing to find steps to a dance none of them knew; how to be together. How to be happy.

The new wife cries a lot, wallows in self-pity. She doesn't know how to live. Her tears seep through the boards into the earth, are sucked down to the place where the last of me lies. I whisper to her as she lies on the cool flags of the kitchen and listens. Soon enough I will rise, making my way upwards as particles of dust; I will settle on her skin, sink into her as I once sank into the earth. I will make her family a foundation upon which they can rely.

Hermione's Farewell

We buried her with a mirror pressed tight against her face, wrapped in place by a scarf.

She had been a queen of two empires. She deserved respect. I painted her face: white lead mixed with gold dust so she would forever be golden. I rimmed her eyes with kohl, then drew the red suns upon her cheeks and chin, so the gods would recognise her when she came before them and know she was one of their own.

Long ago, when she returned to us, she was still beautiful. I knew her by sight, but my own mother had to ask my father who I was. Menelaus himself barely knew. All his attention had been spent chasing her, intent upon dragging her back.

When I was young enough to *want* her love she was an indifferent mother. Later, she was merely dismissive, assured that I was not as beautiful as she was, that no man would launch a war in pursuit of my hand.

Thus I stayed in the shadows, walking quietly so my footfalls did not disturb the gods. My life was overshadowed not just by her loveliness but by its very legend. I hated her, quietly as I did everything, but hated nonetheless.

At last she became ill, felled perhaps by an ill-chosen dish.

I sat by her bedside, dutiful and silent, watching for any sign she might recover. My cousin Orestes had arrived. We had been friends from childhood, and in truth I'd held him in my heart for a long time. But even he watched her, aunt though she was, and she glowed under his attention.

She was glorious still, though weak; inside she was *old*. A cushion over her face was all it took.

I tended her body, pressing the mirror to her face so she would see only herself. So she would not try to leave her body and walk the world once more. So she would not feel alone. Part witch, part goddess—what ordinary grave could hold her? Who thought bright Helen would ever be left in darkness.

As I prepare, now, for my wedding to Orestes, I'm tormented by one thought: no matter that she is gone, she is still in memory. Will always be in memory, mine, Orestes', the world.

Inheritance

"Miss Millikan?"

I can barely hear the woman for the noise in the background at her end. "Yes?"

"It's Nurse Seraph at Sacred Heart. It's your grandmother."

I feel the cold hollow in my stomach, where a vacuum forms. "Has she?"

"Not yet, but you need to come down. The others are here and there's a bit of a problem."

"What sort of a problem?"

"You'll see."

The hospital isn't far. I go on foot. The automatic doors are opening and closing erratically. Ghosts move back and forth just inside.

I take a deep breath and walk through them. They're cold and my clothes feel damp. At the desk, a large nurse is trying to calm down a crowd of old ladies. She sees me, looks relieved.

"Miss Millikan?"

I nod.

"Thank God. She's responsible for this." She gestures at

the spectres. I recognise a couple from sepia-tinted family photos. Uncle Seth looks better dead than alive.

"She's just a little old lady," I lie.

"She's panicking my patients!"

"Okay, okay."

A great line of spirits keeps exiting Vina's room, while she lies on the bed, comatose. My cousins stand around. Tansy sidles up to me, yellow eyes sly. "It's coming out."

Petyr says, "The Inheritance. It's dissipating."

Vala, Arthur, Jezebel and Elizabeth agree.

"Well?" I ask. "I don't want it."

"We *all* have to be here for one to take it," sneers Arthur.

I stare down at the woman who raised us as harshly as she could. We grew up worse than hyenas; no love, no kindness. I don't like them any more than I like her. I tell myself I don't want her inheritance.

"Take it, then, one of you," I say.

They look at each other, then Petyr reaches and my arm, seemingly of its own accord shoots out and beats him. I clamp thumb and forefinger around her nostrils, and cup the other hand across her mouth and hold down tight. She doesn't struggle much. The silver wisps rise from her body slowly, then coalesce into a great silver arrow that shoots into my stomach and knocks me across the room. I cough silver smoke as I sit up.

All the ghosts troop back into the room and politely wait for me to stand. When I do, each steps into me and settles inside the repository of my body. I am the new well of souls.

Lantern

I hear a ship's bell at night, no matter how I block my ears. It's loud as a crying soul. I hear the rush of the sea, too, though this house is landlocked but for the pond and the well. It's all connected, I guess, the water of the world.

We used to live on the coast, once, my father, mother, brother and I, in a cottage by the sea. Simple and sweet until Daffyd came and asked me to walk out with him.

I'd slip into the night, holding the lantern he'd given me. Upon reaching the meeting place I'd slide the cover across the flame three times, no more, no less, so he knew to come from his cottage on the cliffs. I did not know I was sending signals to men and ships alike.

I thought it courting, and I suppose it was, but he was an efficient man, wanting to achieve as many things as possible. Courting me and doing business at the same time appealed to him.

I did not notice for the longest time, while I was infatuated. I did not question his gifts: expensive jewellery and silk dresses sometimes still damp, smelling of salt. While I had his warmth beside me, his face between my hands, and his lips sweet against mine, I did not look out to the wine-dark sea and see ships drawn onto the rocks.

But one night the wind dropped and I heard the bell and turned my head. I saw the ship go aground, watched while smugglers waded into the water. He laboured above me, sweated and swore he loved me while I saw people clubbed like seals.

I pushed him away. He smiled and laughed as he dressed. "You can't tell anyone, sweet accomplice. None will believe you did not know."

I sat up, feeling cold beneath my skin. I felt around for my dress but found instead the lantern. He stood at the edge of the cliff, back to me, assured of my compliance. It flew lightly.

And then there was just the great candle of him, tall and screaming, running off the edge of the cliff. He plummeted like a falling star until the waters embraced him and took him down to meet those he'd sent before.

His voice is lost to the years, but the bell's will not leave me alone.

Red New Day

The chariot awaits, but I cannot leave.

As long as my husband lives he will follow me.

The axe is sharp, bright and washed clean of my sister's old blood. This is the weapon she used against *her* husband, and the one her son used against her in turn. I bade Orestes abandon it when he fled the Furies.

"You will never be free while you carry it."

I hid it for many years, until I had need. It is heavy in my hands, but I swing it, find my rhythm, feel my muscles hum with effort and recognition; I am, after all, a daughter of Sparta.

Though I look not a day over eighteen, I am old. The blood from my father is a god's, but in my bones I feel *old*. The years weigh on me.

I heft the axe again, hear the *whoosh* of it slicing the air, watch the sunlight of the red new day flash against the great double blades. For a moment I am blinded. I think of other battles, other stained weapons.

Memory takes me.

Paris, petulant adolescent, did not like the word 'no'.

When Menelaus left his palace and wife unattended, the Trojan boy struck.

I did not consent, no matter what they say. I did not say "yes". But I took life and limb from seven of them before I was overwhelmed. They dragged me to their ship covered in the blood of others.

And ten years in a gilded cage, rich with Trojan contempt. Watching as the black ships dotted the shore, watching from the high towers as both sides died, all in my name. Until sly Odysseus came, disguised, past rotting corpses the Trojans no longer had the heart to bury. I sent him away with an idea. When at last Menelaus stood there, unable to kill me even though he blamed me, because that would set me free.

In the bottom of the chariot, the scrolls, my history and Troy's; how it burned, its children dashed against stones, its women parcelled out. How its men allowed destruction within its walls.

I take my bright axe and walk to where my husband lies in half-slumber. I think of my sister. I think of escape, of dark caves where I might hide, or shadowy cities where I might wander. I think of my future and it holds shadows.

Seek

Pale and weak, I wake.

Another night of failure.

For a while, I said it wasn't my fault. Nathaniel was too sensitive. Then guilt, that hollow sensation in your heart, in that invisible chamber neither ventricle nor atrium, where feelings reside, seeped in. I thought there would be an echo if someone knocked on me.

Nathaniel ran when he found me with Ben. I remember his devastated blue eyes. It was like he'd cracked inside. He didn't come back. I was certain he was dead.

I had to apologise. To do that I needed the doorway between the living and the dead. So I took to the streets.

The vamps live among the junkies and hookers, all those who fall through. They don't draw attention but everyone knows they're there. Some go to turn, some for the thrill. Others go because the vamps stand one foot on either side of the doorway.

It's hard to find one who will take you right to the edge. A death brings the cops. You need someone who doesn't care.

I don't want to turn. I just need to get *closer*.

I drink juice straight from the bottle. I wolf down stale

danishes: sugar and carbs keep me going. Coffee would make me vibrate.

Outside the sun is turning dark orange, sinking low. I leave the apartment. Last night's suckhead only made me pass out. He wouldn't risk it, but said there was someone who might. A new vamp, bereft of feeling.

The alley is a crack between two buildings. I take a deep breath and enter.

Water pools on the asphalt; moisture seeps down walls. A forgotten dumpster is wedged at the dead-end. It stinks of rotten food.

"Hello? I ..."

What do I say? The previous vamps *knew* what I wanted. Here I feel stupid. Noise, movement behind me; I turn.

Tall, big, the hood of the sweatshirt pulled well down over the face. I swallow.

"What do you want?" A low voice, rough with ill use.

"I want the doorway."

"Why?"

'To... apologise."

He pauses, nods, pushes me against the dumpster. My neck is already dotted with wounds. He drinks deep and quick.

I slip out of my body, see the doorway. I call *Nathaniel*, but there's no answer. I call again, but no one comes.

I drop back into my flesh. He's taking too much. I hit out, dislodge the hood.

Devastated blue eyes flash, my blood bubbles, and soon it's dark.

Sunday Drivers

The dead girl sits in the passenger seat, watching me. Her face is etched with spider-web petichia and her eyes are jelly-red.

My hands are pale and tight at ten and two.

"I'm so sorry, Rachel," I say.

I *really* mean it, not just because I'm in big trouble.

"I cannot *believe*," she spits between blood-stained teeth, "that you slept with my husband."

"It was an accident."

"What, you slipped and fell on it?" It's amazing the volume the dead can reach. I feel a trickle from my ear. My fingers come away red.

"I'm sorry," I whimper.

"Sandy, if you say that again, I'm going to kill you." She deflates. "My own sister."

"I'm – not going to say it again." In front of us the headlights gallop, illuminating the bitumen and the piles of banked-up snow. I should have put the chains on.

"How long?"

"Only a few months." It was more like eighteen, but least said...

"He decided he wanted to be with you so much that he strangled me?"

"Well, maybe he just liked someone who didn't spend all her time in front of the mirror."

"*You* could do with a bit more time in front of the mirror." Recognising the truth, her retort lacks sting.

"There was no need for him to kill you. I really am sorry about that."

"I appreciate you avenging my death," she admits.

Walter hadn't realised that family comes first. He called me to help get rid of Rachel's body. He dropped her into the boot and leaned over to brush hair away from her face. That's when I hit him with the claw-hammer. Seven times. He slumped in on top of her.

Rachel is still talking. "It's almost enough for me to forgive you."

She reaches out. I flinch. Her hand passes through mine like needles of ice. I reef the wheel hard to the left.

The car fishtails, skids, ricochets around the bend and slams into a parked police car with an ear-shattering crash.

I hit my head on the steering wheel, see dark stars. I turn to Rachel, to see if she's *okay*.

She smiles, fading away. "Almost."

There's the "pop" of the trunk and I see the lid rising in the rear-view mirror. Two pissed-off cops clamber out the undamaged side of their vehicle.

I let the darkness flood over me. I'm not going anywhere.

The Impatient Dead

I know more about cemeteries than most people. My mother used to take me weekly to visit my father's grave. My earliest memories are of stone angels and rusting fences. No real feelings beyond a vague sense of having missed out. I do remember my mother, her long dark hair draped around her shoulders like a mourning shawl. If my father was a ghost, my mother was a ragged Ophelia, begging the ground to give up the man she had loved so desperately.

She was mad—what sane woman would take her child to the cemetery with such determination? The unfortunate truth is that madness is hereditary, passed from heart to heart. So it's really no wonder that sooner or later my heart began to resemble my mother's.

She disappeared when I was thirteen. I suppose I lost patience with her. I slipped through life's cracks and made my home among the dead. I grew thin. I ate sadness and drank tears, my soul growing fat and dark. I suppose I was happy. I didn't know I was lonely until I saw him.

After his mother's funeral he stayed, whispering secrets he thought no one else could hear. I lay on the roof of a tomb, listening enchanted, as he poured venom into the grave. Spite and hatred and rage moved in a torrent from his lips and I lost myself in the darkness he summoned.

Here was my twin, the balm for an ache I had not known existed. I wanted to lick him and see if he was poison-flavoured. I wanted him to stay with me and never leave. I thought he would feel the same. I was so convinced that I slithered from my perch and rose up before him.

And he was terrified. He threw rocks at me. One grazed my pale forehead and thick blood started. He ran.

No one takes rejection well. I brought him down before he reached the main gates. I know all the shortcuts—it was easy to play with him.

I dragged him back and threw him into the open maw of a mausoleum. I listened as the shouts grew weaker, the silences grew longer and the whimpering finally ceased. He will not leave me. The dead are impatient for company.

The Problem of Thorns

Around the tower, a wall of thorns, in some places so thick she cannot make out what lies beyond. In a very few spots, she can see grey stone and ravens on an untamed lawn. The road she has taken ends abruptly at the prickly barrier. Left and right, the thorns have melded with the usual flora: she will find no path there. She reaches out to touch one of the branches, but misjudges and snags a finger on a long thorn.

She puts the digit in her mouth, sucks away the welling blood, tastes its metallic tang. The drop of blood remaining on the tip of the thorn gleams then begins to eat away the thorn bush like acid eats at metal. Soon, there is a wound in the wall, big enough for her to walk through. Behind her, the blood continues to erase the thorn bushes as if they never were.

Inside the tower, in a room at the very top of the stairs are the bones, the thread and the canvas of skin, waiting for her touch. On a roughened tabletop lie a quill, a needle and a bottle. At first, she thinks it filled with ink, but closer inspection shows it's a sluggish dark red: blood uncongealed after passing years. She twists the lid; it comes away with surprising ease. The scent of iron stains the air. She feels ill.

The quill is sharp. She picks it up, feels a tingle in her hand, and dips the nib into the blood-ink. She does not hesitate, sketches swiftly the face of the woman who inhabits her dreams. She knows without knowledge that this is her grandmother. The blood-ink soaks straight into the canvas of skin; it knows where it is to stay.

While she waits for the sketch to dry she picks about the tower, trying to find a trail, a story in the left-overs of a life. There is little enough and she realises the only truth here is that of the bones, for the bones remember everything.

She threads the fine silver needle with a long strand of tightly twined flax and black hair. As she stitches, the thread takes on the required colour: ebony black for hair, white as new snow for skin, red as a ripe apple for lips. She stitches and stitches, and wonders what will happen when she is finished.

Things Best Left Alone

I made her swallow it, just before she died. Her eyes were scared, their blue washed pale.

'So you'll come back to me when I call," I told her, avid as a thief.

She was frail, wasted, so light she made no dent on the mattress. Her hair was bleached by the surf, from the days when she would spend hours out on her board, riding the swell, thinking of ways to leave me. It fell out in clumps, staying behind on her pillow when she tried to move, to relieve the ache wading through her flesh.

When at last her eyes rolled back, I picked her up. Her bones were bird-light, made of air.

Four years together and I thought it would never end. We were perfect. She'd loved me for so long without my knowing; when she declared, I was unsure at first, amazed, grateful, bewildered, ecstatic, and finally I believed in nothing but *us*. Why had I not truly *seen* her before? From then on I saw nothing else, everything became peripheral to my obsession: her taste, her touch, her voice, her mind, everything I could mine from her very soul, that became breath to me.

Then she decided to leave me. Said I smothered her, I had

lost myself; she no longer recognised the woman she had loved. That, in being so immersed in her, I had become less than I had been. She found someone else. She thought I didn't hear the furtive phone calls, didn't see the flirty emails becoming love letters.

She stopped noticing me. Didn't see how I started using cosmetics, exercising, trying to look younger. I tried to speak of the clever things I once used to know and embrace, but I found them forgotten; or they had forgotten me and were not forgiving. And I had cast aside my friends long ago.

I carved it of wood, from a tree she had planted, hollowed out the small oval, stuffed in clippings of my hair, dripped in menstrual blood, sealed it up with bees wax and whispered words over it. I cooked all her favourite dishes; watched as she ate. When she started to get sick, she needed *me* again.

Six months ago I laid her in the ground. I've bided my time, letting the need build. I called her tonight, whispered her name, spoke the words, gave them to the breeze to drop on the ground, to seep into her bed of dirt.

It's a moonless night. I hear the door creak, familiar and sad. The bed moves. I smell decay and earth and things best left alone. The bitter taste in my throat may be regret, may be fear. I thought the arsenic would have preserved her better. She slithers across the sheets and settles her rotting flesh against mine, her fetid mouth pressed to my ear and whispers, "I'm home, my love. I came when you called and I'll never leave you."

About the Author

Angela Slatter is the author of *Vigil* (2016), *Corpselight* (2017) and *Restoration* (2018), as well as nine short story collections, including *The Girl with No Hands and Other Tales*, *Sourdough and Other Stories*, *The Bitterwood Bible and Other Recountings*, and *A Feast of Sorrows: Stories*. *Vigil* was nominated for the Dublin Literary Award in 2018.

She has won a World Fantasy Award, a British Fantasy Award, a Ditmar, an Australian Shadows Award and six Aurealis Awards.

Angela's short stories have appeared in Australian, UK and US *Best Of* anthologies such *The Mammoth Book of New Horror*, *The Year's Best Dark Fantasy and Horror*, *The Best Horror of the Year*, *The Year's Best Australian Fantasy and Horror, and The*

Year's Best YA Speculative Fiction. Her work has been translated into Bulgarian, Chinese, Russian, Italian, Spanish, Japanese, Polish, French and Romanian. Victoria Madden of Sweet Potato Films (*The Kettering Incident*) has optioned the film rights to one of her short stories ("Finnegan's Field").

She has an MA and a PhD in Creative Writing, is a graduate of Clarion South 2009 and the Tin House Summer Writers Workshop 2006, and in 2013 she was awarded one of the inaugural Queensland Writers Fellowships. In 2016 Angela was the Established Writer-in-Residence at the Katharine Susannah Prichard Writers Centre in Perth. She has been awarded career development funding by Arts Queensland, the Copyright Agency and, in 2017/18, an Australia Council for the Arts grant.

She is the author of the novellas, *Of Sorrow and Such* (Tor.com) and *Ripper* (in *Horrorology: The Lexicon of Fear*).

Find her online at www.angelaslatter.com

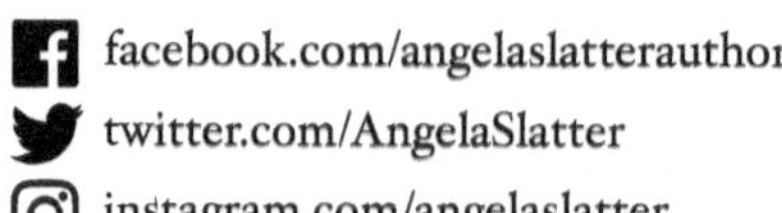

Thank You For Buying This Brain Jar Press Chapbook

To receive special offers, bonus content, and info on
new releases and other great reads, visit us
online at www.BrainJarPress.com

"Jean Bürlesk is a scoundrel and a charlatan. Members of the public are warned not to approach, or he will regale you with the filth and horror he calls *stories*."
Peadar Ó Guilín, award-winning author of *The Call* and *The Invasion*

"Alas, my lawyers have informed me that I have no grounds for a lawsuit against *The Pleasure of Drowning* for trespassing awfully close to the title of my own novel *The Art of Starving*."
Sam J. Miller, Nebula-Award-winning author of *Blackfish City* and *Destroy All Monsters*

"We're sorry we did this to you."
Mr. & Mrs. B... , the author's parents

"... an down demn Hiutt of elena school virus Titel."
Nico Helminger, two-time winner of the Servais Prize, in association with autocorrect

"Jean Bürlesk has been compared to some of the greatest writers in the English language. Mostly by himself, of course, but we think that's fair."
Jean Bürlesk, award-winning author of ... well, this